The Garden Wall

Phyllis Limbacher Tildes

 Charlesbridge

I hated moving day. We drove three hours in morning traffic. I sat in back with Goober and Raisin, my pet mice. Finally Dad said, "This is our street, Tim. We're almost there."

Mom chirped, "Aren't all the houses colorful and pretty?"

All I saw was a lot of look-alike houses squished together. Already I missed the woods, the frog pond, my tree house, and my best friend, Brian. Why did Dad have to take a job in the city?

The moving van was parked in front of our house. Mom rushed up the porch stairs to tell the movers where to put stuff. I was the last one out of the car and into the house.

Our footsteps echoed through the empty rooms. I left the mouse cage in the kitchen and went out to explore the back yard.

Some back yard…one crummy tree and a brick wall. I found a faded rubber ball under a bush and bounced it against the bricks. One really hard throw sent the ball flying over the wall. To my surprise, it came back over. I threw the ball over again. Again it came back.

"Hey, who's there?" I yelled.

Nothing.

"Why don't you answer me?" I was getting angry. A hand waved through an opening then disappeared. I peeked through and saw the big brown eyes of a girl about my age. She giggled and pointed to the far end where the wall was broken. I walked to where I could see her, and wondered what kind of game she was playing.

"Hi. My name is Tim. What's yours?"

She spelled out MARIA in the dirt with a stick. She made strange symbols with her hands and pointed to herself.

Oh, brother. She's deaf! I said to myself. Then I blurted out loud, "Great. I can't even talk to the first kid I meet."

She laughed and nodded yes. Oops! She could read my lips! With a wave of her hand, she invited me to come over the wall and pointed to her house. No way was I going with her! I waved goodbye and ran back to my house thinking, just my luck, my neighbor is not only a girl, but she's deaf too! I sure hope Dad fixes that brick wall.

M A R I A

That day and the next, I worked really hard unpacking and setting up my room. Mom was putting dishes in a cupboard when I pleaded, "PLEASE…can Brian come for a sleepover? Summer vacation is almost over." I was thrilled when Mom said yes. His dad had business in the city and drove Brian the next day.

Brian and I were wrestling in my room when the doorbell rang. I raced him down the stairs and reached the door first. It was Maria.

"Hey, Mom, it's that deaf girl, Maria. She brought us a cake," I yelled.

"Timothy Blake, where are your manners?" scolded Mom as she came down the hall. "Invite her in."

Once inside, Maria handed the cake and a card to Mom. Maria didn't look too happy. I'll bet her mother made her come over. The note welcomed us to the neighborhood. Mom said, "How thoughtful. Tim, why don't you show Maria your room while I write a reply to her mother?"

I rolled my eyes and stomped up the stairs with Brian. After Mom smiled and waved her hand toward the stairs, Maria followed.

"Your girlfriend sure is quiet. Quiet as a mouse," Brian teased.

"She can understand what you say, dummy! She reads lips!" I replied.

Maria ignored Brian. She was more interested in my mice. I opened the cage and put Raisin in her hand. I started playing action figures with Brian. We hardly noticed her putting the mouse back in the cage and leaving.

The following Monday was the first day of school. I was dreading it. I could hardly eat my French toast. We saw Maria walk past the house and meet up with another girl.

"I wonder if Maria will be in your class," Mom said.

I hope not, I thought. "How can a deaf kid go to my school?" I asked.

"I'm sure some of the teachers can sign, and there are sign language interpreters to help them," she explained. "Now, off you go. Have a great day. I know you will make lots of new friends."

During the five-block walk, cars honked, sirens roared, and trucks screeched. I could see Maria and her friend ahead of me. Every now and then, they turned to look at me and giggle.

The old brick building on the corner of Broad Street and 23rd had big green double doors that seemed to swallow all the students running up the steps. I followed the crowd in and found my way to Miss Alpert's class in room 102.

She introduced me to the students and welcomed me to Broad Street School. I took a seat two rows back from Maria.

I was amazed that a few kids knew some sign language and were able to "talk" to Maria. Miss Alpert knew some too, but depended on Mrs. Chen, the interpreter. We all learned that the next day would be Show and Tell Day. I knew what I would bring.

When I walked into class on Tuesday with Goober and Raisin, everyone crowded around me. They begged me to take one of the mice out of the cage before class began. While I was holding Goober, Izzie Thornton bulldozed his way through the group and grabbed the mouse. Hanging Goober by his tail he said, "What a good snack for my boa constrictor!"

I froze, but Maria jumped up to snatch Goober from Izzie. The mouse dropped to the floor and scurried under a bookcase. I tried to coax Goober out. No luck. Class began and I could tell my "Show" was already over.

During recess I tried to find Goober again. I was surprised when Maria offered to help. She put some cheese from her lunch near the bookcase. Soon Goober came out to munch. When I picked him up Maria made a sign with her hands.

"Mouse?" I guessed. She nodded yes. I put Goober back with Raisin and tried making the sign.

She showed me how to sign my name, too. She sure was being nice after I had tried to ignore her.

mouse

T   I   M

Later that week we studied fables. We had to pair up and choose a fable to perform in two weeks. When Miss Alpert suggested that Maria and I work together, I was silent. What could I say? How was I going to do a project with a girl I couldn't even talk with?

I guess Maria was hurt and angry when she saw the look on my face. She signed something to the teacher. "Maria says maybe you would rather have Izzie as a partner, Tim."

I said, "No, Maria would be okay."

Maria didn't look too thrilled with me either, but she wrote, Let's do the story of *The Town Mouse and the Country Mouse*. We can plan and rehearse at my house.

Great. Now I had to go to her house after all.

The next afternoon I rang Maria's doorbell. When she answered the door, I wondered how she could have heard the bell. Later I learned that a light blinks when it rings.

I followed Maria into the kitchen. She stomped on the floor to get her mother's attention. That seemed rude until I figured out her mother was deaf too. Mrs. Delgado turned and waved hello. She offered me some cookies.

The phone rang and flashed a bright light. Maria ran to answer the phone. It was for her, so she started typing a reply.

While I nibbled on a cookie, Maria's mother continued to make supper. Cupboards opened and closed with a bang. Drawers slammed shut. The TV in the corner had subtitles. It was turned up way too loud. A house with deaf people could be really noisy.

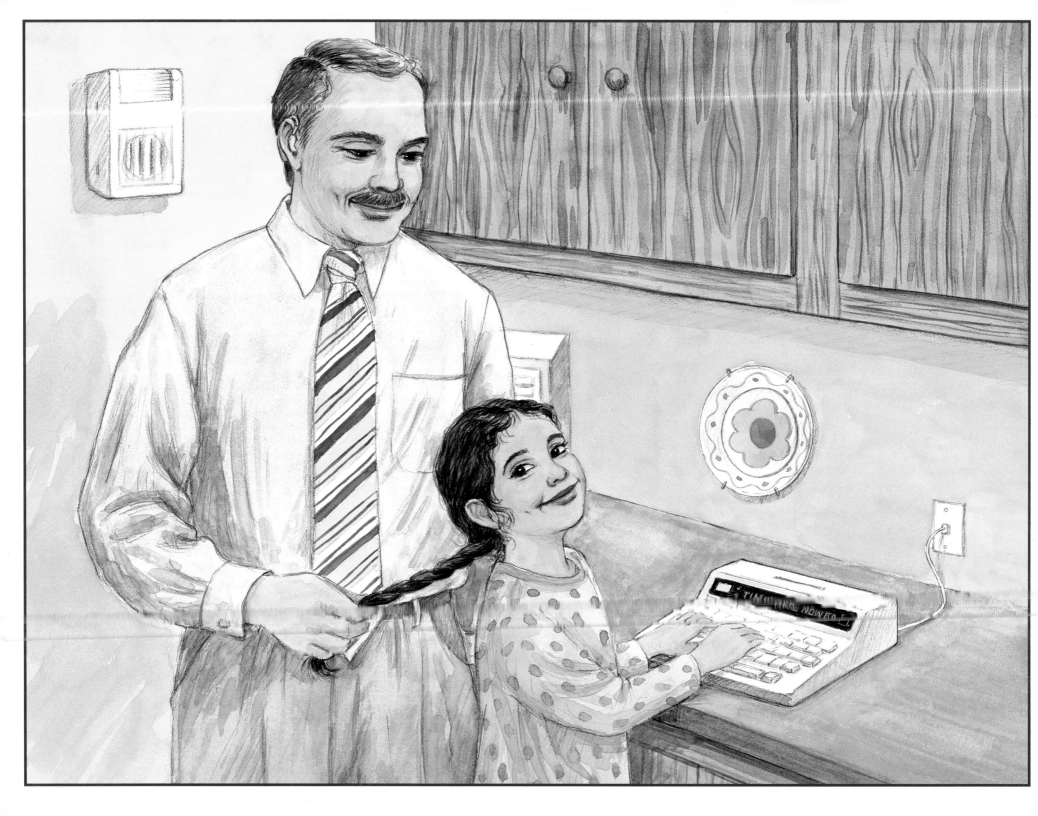

Footsteps rumbled down the hall and Mr. Delgado burst into the kitchen. He gave Maria's braid a playful tug. Like my grandfather, he wore a hearing aid and spoke out loud. He offered to help us communicate our ideas with each other as we started on our project.

Phew! That was a relief.

When Maria finished her call we worked out our roles. She was kind of bossy and insisted that I should be a Hearing Country Mouse and she a Deaf Town Mouse. I would speak both our parts and she would sign. She wanted to dance her part to music, too. I asked how she could "hear" the music.

Maria slipped a CD into the player. Music shook the room as she danced around.

"She feels the vibration in the floor...especially drums and bass," her father explained. When he suggested I dance with Maria, she quickly turned the music off. Good thing!

We rehearsed for many days. I have to admit, I actually looked forward to it. Teaming up with Maria was kind of neat. She taught me a few more words in sign language and most of the signing alphabet. It was fun…like a secret code. She even gave me a name sign. It's like a nickname in sign language. Mine is a hand-shape letter "T" touching the side of the forehead.

On the day of the play, we were the fourth to perform. My heart was pounding and my hand shook as I painted squiggly whiskers on Maria's face. She didn't seem at all nervous. At least *she* didn't have to talk!

I sort of squeaked my first lines, and I wasn't even trying to sound mousy! "Work, work, work from sun-up to sun-down. Wouldn't life be better in town? No animals to feed, no garden to tend. I wonder what my deaf cousin's town house is like?"

Tim

When the music started, Maria danced as she dusted her town house, acting in mime and sign. I spoke what she signed. "The city is so dirty. Life would be better in the country. I'm going to visit my hearing country cousin."

The play went smoothly as we visited each other's homes, only to learn our own place was best. The Deaf Town Mouse missed her flashing doorbell, special telephone, and vibrating alarm clock. And she didn't like feeding farm animals. The Hearing Country Mouse was confused by the flashing lights, hated the noises of the city and missed the fresh country air.

All the kids (even Izzie) clapped and waved their hands in the air, which is the way to applaud a deaf person. I was glad it was over.

After school I saw Maria walking home alone. I ran to catch up to her. She smiled at me and pointed to herself and me. Then she made a sign linking her two forefingers together.

"Friends?" I guessed. She smiled again and nodded. I just looked down at my feet and continued walking beside her.

Later that afternoon I met Maria at the end of our garden wall. I made the sign for "friends." Her brown eyes sparkled as she reached across the broken wall and linked her forefinger in mine.

I was glad there wasn't a wall between us after all.

friends

American Manual Alphabet

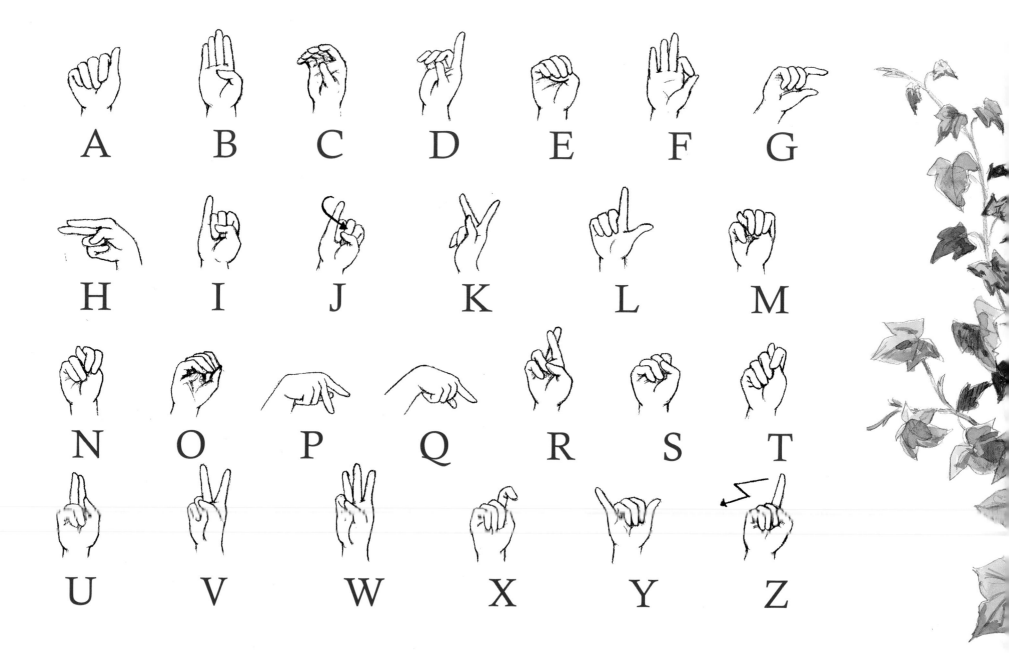

In 2001 *Imagination Stage's* Deaf Access Program created a successful stage production of my book, *The Magic Babushka*. It was a thrill to see my story come to life through the spoken word, signing, costumes, sets, and innovation of this vital youth program. *Imagination Stage* of Bethesda, Maryland is nationally recognized for increasing the public awareness of the culture of the deaf through theater productions in which both deaf and hearing students perform.

I was delighted when Bonnie Fogel, founder and executive director of *Imagination Stage*, asked to collaborate with me on a story about the developing friendship between a deaf child and hearing child.

I want to express my appreciation to Bonnie Fogel and Deaf Access Directors Lisa Agogliati and Donna Salamoff for their insight and help in creating the story, *The Garden Wall*.

Phyllis L. Tildes

To learn more about Imagination Stage, *you may contact the directors at their exciting, new regional children's center:* 4908 Auburn Avenue, Bethesda, MD 20814
(301) 961-6060
www.imaginationstage.org

*For all the student performers
of Imagination Stage,
past, present, and future.*

—P. L. T.

2006 First hardcover edition
Text and illustrations copyright © 2005 by Phyllis Limbacher Tildes

Published by Charlesbridge
85 Main Street
Watertown, MA 02472
(617) 926-0329
www.charlesbridge.com

Developed in cooperation with the Deaf Access Program at Imagination Stage, Inc., Bethesda, Maryland.

The contents of this book were developed under a grant from the Department of Education.
However, those contents do not necessarily represent the policy of the Department of Education,
and you should not assume endorsement by the Federal Government.

Library of Congress Cataloging-in-Publication Data
Tildes, Phyllis Limbacher.
   The garden wall / Phyllis Limbacher Tildes.
      p. cm.
   Summary: Already unhappy that his family has moved from the country
to the city, Tim is not pleased when his new neighbor turns out to be
not only a girl, but also deaf.
   ISBN-13: 978-1-57091-467-6; ISBN-10: 1-57091-467-2 (reinforced for library use)
   ISBN-13: 978-1-57091-468-3; ISBN-10: 1-57091-468-0 (softcover)
[1. Deaf—Fiction. 2. Friendship—Fiction. 3. Moving, Household—Fiction.
4. City and town life—Fiction. 5. People with disabilities—Fiction. 6.
School—Fiction.] I. Title.
PZ7.T4559Gar 2007
[Fic]—dc22   2005035814

Printed in Korea
(hc) 10 9 8 7 6 5 4 3 2 1
(sc) 10 9 8 7 6 5 4 3 2 1

Illustrations done in watercolor and pencil
Display type and text type set in Calisto MT
Color separations by Friesens in Canada through Four Colour Imports Ltd., Louisville, Kentucky
Printed and bound by Sung In Printing, South Korea
Production supervision by Brian G. Walker